THE HAT

Carol Ann Duffy lives in Manchester with her
eleven-year-old daughter, Ella, and grew up in Stafford.
She has published seven collections of poems for adults
and has received many awards. She won the 1993
Whitbread Award for Poetry and the Forward Prize for
best collection for *Mean Time*. *The World's Wife* received
the E. M. Forster Award in America; *Rapture*, the T. S.
Eliot Prize in Britain. Her first collection of poems for
children, *Meeting Midnight*, was shortlisted for the
Whitbread Children's Book of the Year in 1999, and
her second, *The Oldest Girl in the World*, received the
Signal Prize for Children's Poetry.

by the same author

for children
GRIMM TALES
MORE GRIMM TALES
(both adapted from the Brothers Grimm and dramatised by Tim
Supple for the Young Vic Theatre Company)
RUMPELSTILTSKIN AND OTHER GRIMM TALES
MEETING MIDNIGHT
THE OLDEST GIRL IN THE WORLD
UNDERWATER FARMYARD
QUEEN MUNCH AND QUEEN NIBBLE
THE SKIPPING-ROPE SNAKE
THE GOOD CHILD'S GUIDE TO ROCK'N'ROLL
THE STOLEN CHILDHOOD AND OTHER DARK FAIRY TALES
DORIS THE GIANT
MOON ZOO
BEASTS AND BEAUTIES
THE LOST HAPPY ENDINGS

for adults
STANDING FEMALE NUDE
SELLING MANHATTAN
THE OTHER COUNTRY
MEAN TIME
SELECTED POEMS
THE WORLD'S WIFE
FEMININE GOSPELS
NEW SELECTED POEMS
RAPTURE

as editor
I WOULDN'T THANK YOU FOR A VALENTINE
STOPPING FOR DEATH
TIME'S TIDINGS
HAND IN HAND
OVERHEARD ON A SALTMARSH
OUT OF FASHION
ANSWERING BACK

THE HAT

CAROL ANN DUFFY

Illustrations by
DAVID WHITTLE

faber and faber

First published in 2007
by Faber and Faber Limited
3 Queen Square London WC1N 3AU

Design by Mandy Norman
Printed in England by Mackays of Chatham, plc

A CIP record for this book
is available from the British Library

ISBN 978–0–571–21965–0

2 4 6 8 10 9 7 5 3 1

FOR ELLA WITH LOVE FROM MUMMY

CONTENTS

THE
SONG
COLLECTOR

The first song I gathered was that of a man locked up
in a cell, who sang to the mournful toll of the prison bell
as I walked by: *This morning I'm going to die, to die,*
and only the girl who loved me once knows why.

The second song was sung by a lad in a lane
where I swayed on a stile, swigging my ale,
so I asked him to sing it again for a coin and he did:
This is simply the simple song of a simple kid.

Song three was trilled by a bunch of nuns – that
was a Latin one, *dominus, dominum* – outside a church,
and four, five, six, I picked from a farm, eye-high
in corn, as I chanced my tattooed arm at harvesting.

Stopped counting then, when I got to ten, and the next
I knew I had more than a few to my repertoire;
so I bought a guitar, played four to the bar, wandered
wide and far, with an ear for a humming lad or a yodelling girl.

With an ear for a whistling train, for a foghorn ship.
With an ear for percussion rain, for the tune the wind blows
through the trees. With an ear for the birds and bees,
yippees, for quavers, crotchets, minims, doh ray me's.

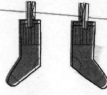

THE
SOCK

Most feet stink
and those that don't,
unfortunately,
pong.

Dang ding.
Dang ding.
Dang ding.
Dang ding dong.

You wouldn't think
there's much
to being a sock.
You would be wrong.

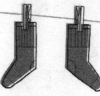

Dang ding.
Dang ding.
Dang ding.
Dang ding dong.

What's dang?
What's ding?
You're asking.
It's my song.

Dang ding.
Dang ding.
Dang ding.
Dang ding dong.

SONG

As I walked in a garden green
I heard a singing girl,
her song a sure and silver line
which pulled me from the world
to where she sat, the flowers wild,
crooning to a little child –
Lull, lully, lully, lulla lay,
all words are living flesh today,
lull, lully, lalla lay.

I sat down underneath a tree.
For thirty years I'd walked
dragging my shadow after me
and never heard it talk,
but now it sighed upon the grass –
a child, a girl, is born today
and she is yours to take away,
lull, lully lully, lulla lay,
lull, lully, lalla lay.

My shadow turned into a babe.
I turned into a girl.
The song I sang was new to me,
yet I knew every word
and rocked the infant in my arms,
keeping her from harm.
Lull, lully, lully, lulla lay,
all words are living flesh today,
lull, lully, lalla lay.

ROOTY TOOTY

Grandad used to be a pop star,
with a red-and-silver guitar.
He wore leather jackets and drainpipe jeans.
He drove around in limousines,
waving to screaming fans.
Fab! said Grandad. *Groovy!*
I really dig it, man!

Grandad used to have real hips,
he swivelled and did The Twist.
His record went to Number One.
Grandad went like this:
Rooty tooty, yeah yeah.
Rooty tooty, yeah yeah.
Rooty tooty, yeah yeah.
Then Grandad met Gran.

Gran was dancing under a glitterball.
Grandad was on bass.
He noticed how a thousand stars
sparkled and shone in her face.
And although Gran fancied the drummer,
Grandad persevered. He wrote Gran
a hundred love songs
down through their happy years.

Grandad used to be a pop star,
a rock'n'roll man –
Rooty tooty, yeah yeah yeah –
and Grandad loved groovy Gran.

# TOUCHED

A ghost touched me. Elizabeth Norris. Don't laugh.
It's true; her hand on my cheek, cool as a flannel
dropped in a drained bath.

                   Felt by a ghost, me;
don't grin. I nearly screamed – chill fingers
under my chin, a sister of ice, she,
coaxing me in,

             in, to the cold space
of her past. I gasped as she read my lips
with her fingertips, Tudor, dead, laid her head
on my shoulder

             like a sad friend. Poor Elizabeth,
she touched me, here, in my heart – for how, now,
though we never met, could we ever part?

QUEEN'S BEES

In Elizabethan times, it was considered lucky to tell bees gossip otherwise they would leave.

The Queen told the bees
it was Henry VIII she mourned.
Grieving, they swarmed.

The Queen told the bees
of the axe at the throat of her mother.
They swooned in the clover.

The Queen told the bees
there was no man living she'd love.
Smitten, they buzzed.

The Queen told the bees
the names of those sent to the Tower.
They prayed at their flowers.

The Queen told the bees
of the rack, the thumbscrew, the whip.
Frenzied, they sipped.

The Queen told the bees
that the head of Queen Mary had fallen.
They cheered and huzzahed in the pollen.

HOW MANY
SAILORS
TO SAIL A SHIP?

One with a broken heart
to weep sad buckets.

Two with four blue eyes
to mirror the sea.

One with a salty tongue
to swear at a pirate.

Two with four green eyes
to mirror the sea.

One with a wooden leg
to dance on a gang-plank.

Two with four grey eyes
to mirror the sea.

Luff! Leech! Clew! Tack!
Off to sea! Won't be back!

One with an arrowed heart
tattooed on a bicep.

Two with four blue eyes
to mirror the sky.

One with a baby's caul
to keep from a-drowning.

Two with four grey eyes
to mirror the sky.

One with a flask of rum
to gargle at midnight.

Two with four black eyes
to mirror the sky.

Luff! Clew! Tack! Leech!
Off to sea! No more beach!

One with an albatross
to put in a poem.

Two with four blue eyes
to mirror the sea.

One with a secret map
to stitch in a lining.

Two with four grey eyes
to mirror the sea.

One with a violin
to scrape at a dolphin.

Two with four green eyes
to mirror the sea.

Luff! Leech! Tack! Clew!
Off to sea! Yo ho! Adieu!

One with a telescope
to clock the horizon.

Two with four blue eyes
to mirror the sky.

One with a yard of rope
to lasso a tempest.

Two with four grey eyes
to mirror the sky.

One with a heavy heart
to sink for an anchor.

Two with four black eyes
to mirror the sky.

Leech! Clew! Tack! Luff!
Off to sea! We've had enough!
Luff! Leech! Tack! Clew!
Off to sea! Yo ho! Adieu!

THE
OCEAN'S
BLANKET

The ocean's blanket is made of dark green seaweed
and golden mermaids' hair.
We see a thousand starfish there.

The ocean's blanket is made of crashing waves
and frothy, creamy foam.
It keeps us warm.

The ocean's blanket is made of smiling dolphins
and lonely, singing whales.
We see the silver of the fishes scales.

The ocean's blanket is made of waltzing octopuses
and dancing, inky squid.
It keeps us hid.

The ocean's blanket is made of hidden pearls
and spicy, salty smells.
We see the jewels of a million shells.

The ocean's blanket is made of sunken ships
and we are drowned, are drowned.
Beneath the ocean's blanket we will not be found.

I believe in sand
because of its thousand whispers
held in my hands,

because of a starfish
worn like a brooch
and earring shells,

and the way it frowns
when the tide goes out,
and its seaweed smell.

I believe in sand
because of its magic castle
made by my hands,

because of a name
scored with a stick
at the edge of the tide,

and the salty lace
at the throat of a wave
where dolphins ride.

I believe in sand
because of the secret water
dug by my hands,

because of the footprints
leading away, leading away
to other lands,
I believe in sand.

She wouldn't say *Boo!* to a goose.
But she played cards with a puss
and gambled her dosh.

She wouldn't say *Boo!* to a goose.
But she went out to dine with a grouse
at the Hotel de Posh.

She wouldn't say *Boo!* to a goose.
But she danced all night with a moose
by the light of the moon.

She wouldn't say *Boo!* to a goose.
But she supped with a couple of newts
from a golden spoon.

She wouldn't say *Boo!* to a goose.
But she rode on the back of a mouse
in a field of corn.

She wouldn't say *Boo!* to a goose.
But she haunted a house with a ghost
from dusk till dawn.

But she wouldn't say *Boo!*
She wouldn't say *Boo!*
She wouldn't say *Boo!* to a goose.

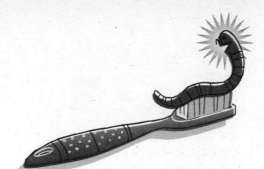

BE VERY
AFRAID

of the Spotted Pyjama Spider
which disguises itself as a spot
on the sleeve of your nightwear,
waits till you fall asleep,
then commences its ominous creep
towards your face.

Be very afraid
of the Hanging Lightcord Snake
which waits in the dark
for your hand to reach for the switch,
then wraps itself round your wrist
with a venomous hiss. Be afraid,

very afraid, of the Toothpaste Worm
which is camouflaged as a stripe of red
in the paste you squeeze
and oozes onto your brush
with a wormy guile
to squirm on your smile.

Be very afraid indeed
of the Bookworm Bat
which wraps itself like a dust-jacket
over a book,
then flaps and squeaks in your face
when you take a look. Be afraid

of the Hairbrush Rat, of the Merit Badge Beetle,
of the Bubble Bath Jellyfish
and the Wrist Watch Tick (with its terrible nip),
of the Sock Wasp, of the Bee in the Bonnet
(posed as an amber jewel
in the hatpin on it). Be feart

of the Toilet Roll Scorpion,
snug as a bug in its cardboard tube
until someone disturbs it,
of the Killer Earring Ant,
dangling from a lobe
until someone perturbs it. Don't be brave –

be very afraid.

TALES OF THE EXPECTED

1   *The Monster of Ghosty Bog*

When a sudden mist swirled in from the sea
to muffle and blindfold the town,
those who were out – and I was one –
hurried for home, hoods up, heads down.

Legend claimed that the Monster of Ghosty Bog
would prowl through the salty fog, ravenous,
in search of a kid to bite and gobble and chew.
The townsfolk would find a little bone next day,

a sock or a shoe, a muddy toy . . . no girl or boy
was safe when the mist boiled in from the waves
to poach the wriggling town. The Monster would pin
you down! The Monster would suck your eyes

like boiled sweets! The Monster would leave your brains
on the side of the street! Beware! Take care!
Parents who let their child play out would soon come
to grieve it. So legend had it. But no one believed it.

2   Ghoul School

The Headmaster isn't a vampire.
He doesn't drink blood,
or sleep in a coffiny bed
with a duvet of mud.

The Deputy Head's no werewolf.
She doesn't noisily eat
the Infants for hors d'oeuvres
and the Juniors for sweet.

The teachers aren't ghouls.
Their yellow teeth don't bite
the trembling hands of pupils
learning to read and write.

The school isn't a ghost ship
floating away from the town . . .
nobody left on board . . .
a bell ringing for the drowned.

3   The Dark

If you think of the dark
as a black park
and the moon as a bounced ball,
then there's nothing to be frightened of
at all.

(Except for aliens . . .)

CRIKEY DICK

I've eaten too much chocolate, I feel sick.
The stink of snuffed-out candles gets my wick.
There's a scab upon my knee I want to pick.
I cannot do my homework, I'm too thick.
There's only one thing for it – CRIKEY DICK!

I've stuffed myself with pizza, now I'm ill.
My mark out of a hundred's always nil.
The medicine I take's a bitter pill.
I feel so stressed although I want to chill.
There's only one thing for it – BLIMEY PHIL!

There's never any ink inside my pen.
There's never any Nevis on my Ben.
There's never any egg inside my hen.
I stop at seven when I count to ten.
There's only one thing for it – LUMME LEN!

There's only one thing for it – LUMME LEN!
There's only one thing for it – BLIMEY PHIL!
So when you feel like shouting BLOODY HELL!
or smashing through a window with a brick –
there's only one thing for it – CRIKEY DICK!

WAS A LAD

We didn't eat sweets when I was a lad,
we ate dust.
We walked on our feets when I was a lad,
there was no bus.
There was no fuss when I was a lad,
no fuss.

We didn't wear clothes when I was a lad,
we wore rags.
We had no shoes when I was a lad,
we had clogs.
There were no hugs when I was a lad,
no hugs.

We didn't play games when I was a lad,
we played dead.
We had no names when I was a lad,
there was no need.
There was no bread when I was a lad,
no bread.

We didn't drink Coke when I was a lad,
we drank rain.
We never felt sick when I was a lad,
there was no pain.
There was no phone when I was a lad,
no phone.

We didn't we never when I was a lad,
we had no say.
We hadn't we couldn't when I was a lad,
there was no pay.
There wasn't we shouldn't when I was a lad,
no way.

YOUR
DRESSES

I like your rain dress,
its strange, sad colour,
its small buttons like tears.

I like your fog dress,
how it swirls around you
when you dance on the lawn.

Your snow dress I like,
its million snowflakes
sewn together with a needle of ice.

But I love your thunderstorm dress,
its huge, dark petticoats,
its silver stitches flashing as you run away.

PERHAPS

Perhaps a cloud, folded to
the four white squares of a handkerchief;

or a fistful of stars, dropped
in your purse for pocket money.

Perhaps a hurricane, smoothed
and hammered to a brooch;

or a field of grass, pleated,
hemmed and zipped for a kilt.

Perhaps a river, buckled
with bright, pewtery fish, for a belt;

or a rainbow, unpicked
to seven ribbons for your hair.

Perhaps the sea, flounced
and gathered into petticoats;

or the moon, framed, hung on your wall
for a mirror – look how lovely you are!

THE
LOOK

The heron's the look of the river.
The moon's the look of the night.
The sky's the look of forever.
Snow is the look of white.

The bees are the look of the honey.
The wasp is the look of pain.
The clown is the look of funny.
Puddles are the look of rain.

The whale is the look of the ocean.
The grave is the look of the dead.
The wheel is the look of motion.
Blood is the look of red.

The rose is the look of the garden.
The girl is the look of the school.
The snake is the look of the Gorgon.
Ice is the look of cool.

The clouds are the look of the weather.
The hand is the look of the glove.
The bird is the look of the feather.
You are the look of love.

LOVING

Go slow,
come soon,
eyes meet
on the moon.

Me here,
you far,
eyes meet
at a star.

Dark space
between us,
eyes meet
at Venus.

PAY ME IN
LIGHT

Pay me in light,
the sun's bonanza
flung in handfuls through the trees,
amber in green leaves; pay me
in the silver lining of the clouds,
a percentage of rain.

Pay me in light,
the newly minted moon,
the small-change stars,
the precious galaxy
sieved from space like gold,
a solitaire tear.

Pay me in light,
a candle's tongue in the dark's cheek,
sapphire lightning as we run for home,
your hand in mine, warm
as a small flame,
through lucky jackpot hail.

MRS HAMILTON'S
REGISTER

Grace and beauty?
Annie, here.
Eternal blossom?
Amarachi, here.
Celestial spirit?
Devashree, here.
One to admire?

Emily, here.

Light of a girl?

Ella, here.

Heaven's benevolence?

Gianina, here.

Hill near meadows?

Georgina, here.

Kind angel?

Juanaya, here.

Sea of riches?

Molly, here.

Victorious heart?

Nicola, here.

Little one?

Polly, here.

Lovely flower?

Rosie, here.

Twilight hour?

Sharvari, here.

Soft dark eyes?

Siya, here.

Thank you, girls.

Thank you, Mrs Hamilton.

THE LAUGH OF YOUR CLASS

Your class laughs like fourteen birds
in a tree.
Your class laughs like ice in a glass
on a tray.
Your class laughs like the stars
in the Milky Way.
Ha ha ha ha ha ho ho hee hee.

Your class laughs like the horn
of a bright red car.
Your class laughs like the strings
on a loud guitar.
Your class laughs like the harmony
of a choir.
Ho ho ho ho ho hee hee ha ha.

Your class laughs like the hiss
of skis on snow.
Your class laughs like the screams
at a circus show.
Your class laughs like a trumpet player's
blow.
Hee hee hee hee hee ha ha ho ho.

Your class laughs like fourteen seals
in the sea.
Your class laughs like a drunken
chimpanzee.
Your class laughs like the buzz
of a honey bee.
Ha ha ha ha ha ho ho hee hee.

Your class laughs like the mighty
ocean's roar.
Your class laughs like carol singers
at the door.
Your class laughs like an elephant
in the shower.
Ho ho ho ho ho hee hee ha ha.

Your class laughs like doh ray me
fa so.
Your class laughs like seven dwarves singing
hi ho.
Your class laughs like blue whales
when they blow.
Hee hee hee hee hee ha ha ho ho.
Ha ha ha ha ha ho ho hee hee.
Ho ho ho ho ho hee hee ha ha.
Hee hee hee hee hee ha ha ho ho.

I ADORE
YEAR 3

I went past their door.
I went past their door.
They were asleep on the floor!
Year 4.

I went past their door.
I went past their door.
I heard them all snore!
Year 4.

I went past their door.
I went past their door.
It must be a bore!
Year 4.

I went past their door.
I went past their door.
I want to ignore
Year 4.

I went past their door.
I went past their door.
The future I saw!
Year 4.

Year 3 I adore!
Year 3! I want more —
Till I go through the door
Till I (Aaagh!) go through the door
Till I go (No! No!) through the door
of Year 4.

ASK
OSCAR

Dear Oscar,
I stay up too late
the night before an exam
trying to cram.
What do you advise?

Revise.

Dear Oscar,
I have fallen in love
with a girl in my class at school.
I feel such a fool!
What should I do?

Woo.

Dear Oscar,
I am prone to spots – lots!
What can you suggest please?

Squeeze.

Dear Oscar,
I keep seeing a ghost
on the stairs.
Are ghosts real
or am I being foolish?

Ghoulish.

Dear Oscar,
there are so many faiths
in the world.
Which, in your view,
is The One?

None.

Dear Oscar,
I want to be a poet!
Please tell me how
if you can spare the time.

Rhyme.

NOT NOT NURSERY RHYMES

1 Cool, Kind Buns

Cool, kind buns.
Cool, kind buns.
Very many?
Hardly any
Cool, kind buns.

2 Three Sharp-Sighted Mice

Three sharp-sighted mice,
Three sharp-sighted mice.
See how they run!
See how they run!
They're all avoiding the farmer's wife –
She's slit his throat with a carving knife.
They've never seen so much blood in their life –
Those three sharp-sighted mice.

3   Humpty Dumpty

Humpty Dumpty stood on one leg.
Humpty Dumpty was only an egg.
All the King's horses
And all the King's men
Had to have omelette for dinner again.

4   Jack and Jill

Jill and Jill went up the hill
To fetch themselves a daughter.
Jack and Jack were coming back,
And all of them did what they oughta.

5   Ho Doodle Doodle

Ho doodle doodle,
The rat and the poodle
Were quarrelling over a bone.
An elephant came
and told me their game
in a text from its mobile phone.

THE
ALPHABEST

Aye! to avocados stuffed with prawns.

Bravo! to bowling on smooth green lawns.

Cool! to Christmas and Santa Claus.

Delightful! to dogs who extend their paws.

Encore! to everyone who takes the stage.

Fab! to the fairy on the storybook page.

Gorgeous! to the girl in designer jeans.

Hurrah! to the heir of the reigning queen.

I likey! to the ice cream dripping down my cone.

Jolly good! to the jacket on my mobile phone.

Kiss! to the kid with the Kiss-Me-Quick hat.

Lovely! to the lady with the sleek black cat.

Marvellous! to mushy peas with fish and chips.

Nice one! to the number on the winning slip.

OK! to the owner of a brand new car.

Perfect! to the pop star with the loud guitar.

Quintessential! to the queue for a bestselling book.

Respect! to the rapper with the coolest look.

Smashing! to sextuplets on a mother's knee.

Tops! to the thrush singing in the tree.

Up! with umbrellas in springtime rain.

Vote! for Vegetarians Against Animal Pain.

Wicked! to waffles with chocolate sauce.

Xcellent! to XXX (means I love you, of course).

Yes! to the yellow of a soft-boiled egg.

Zooper-dooper! to the zoo with the dinosaur egg.

THE
MANCHESTER
COWS

1   Arrival

Cows arrived.
Clouds stopped raining.
Crowds of people
stopped complaining.

2   Harvey Nicks

A girl called
Annabel Jessica Pickles
bumped into a cow
in Harvey Nichols.

3 Chinatown

A gentle cow
in Chinatown
ate steamed har kau,
washed it down
with jasmine tea,
then for pudding
had lychee.

4 School

At Manchester High School for Cows,
the favourite lesson is Mooing –
they all make a terrible row,
then its off down to lunch for some Chewing.

5   Shopping

The cow in Oilily was silly.
The cow in Jigsaw was RUDE.
In Daisy and Tom, the cow sang a song
(or tried to – it really just mooed).

6   Colours

A red cow
stands in goal
at Old Trafford.

Outside the City Art Gallery
a creamy cubist cow
dreams of Picasso.

A yellow cow
ambles down the Curry Mile
under a harvest moon.

The pink cow
in Didsbury Village
is GORGEOUS –
and knows it.

The sad blue cow
stands in the Southern Cemetery rain
till love, till love,
returns again.

7 Creatures

Six silly cows
on a hen night
at a zebra crossing.

8 Haikow

Moo moo moo moo moo,
Moo moo moo moo moo moo moo,
Moo moo moo moo moo.

9   Great Cow Artists

PICOWSSO

MOONET

MICHELANGELOW

CONSTABLE

MOODIGLIANI

MOOTISSE

LEONARDO BAA VINCI (he was a sheep, actually)

EDVARD MOONCH (his most famous painting is *The Cream*)

OSCAR COWKOSCHKA

EL GRECOW

FRIDA COWLO

10 Best Friend

If my best friend was a cow,
her hide would feel like silk,
and she'd be full of lemonade,
not milk.
      Her udders would be bagpipes,
they'd play a Scottish tune,
and we'd dance together,
two daft cows,
then jump right over the moon.

11 Hotel

Two cows swanned into
the Midland Hotel,
all dressed up
and wearing bells;
had tea and toast –
'what fun!' they said –
then took the lift
and went to bed.

A STICK INSECT'S FUNERAL POEM

(co-written with Ella Duffy)

Goodbye, Courgette,
insect pet.
You are old and cold.

Goodbye, Courgette,
I won't forget
how tickly you were to hold.

Goodbye, Courgette,
the best pet.
I love you so, like gold.

Oh, Courgette!

THE FRUITS,
THE VEGETABLES,
THE FLOWERS
AND THE TREES

1   *The Fruits*

Which is the most friendly of the fruits?

Is it the apple?

No, for the apple is the most romantic of the fruits.

Is it the apricot?

No, for the apricot is the most self-concious of the fruits.

Then is it the cherry?

No, for the cherry is the most cheerful of the fruits.

Then is it the raspberry?

No, for the raspberry if the most rude of the fruits.

Perhaps it is the quince?

No, for the quince is the most ironic of the fruits.

Perhaps it is the grape?

No, for the grape is the most healing of the fruits.

Is it the damson?

No, for the damson is the most particular of the fruits.

Is it the fig?

No, for the fig is the most demure of the fruits.

Then is it the Victoria plum?

No, for the Victoria plum is the most solemn of the fruits.

Then is it the kumquat?

No, for the kumquat is the most clever of the fruits.

Perhaps it is the pineapple?

No, for the pineapple is the most spiteful of the fruits.

Perhaps it is the lemon?

No, for the lemon is the most naive of the fruits.

Is it the melon?

No, for the melon is the most optimistic of the fruits.

Is it the orange?

No, for the orange is the most gregarious of the fruits.

Then is it the ugli fruit?

No, for the ugli fruit is the most intellectual of the fruits.

Then is it the tangerine?

No, for the tangerine is the most festive of the fruits.

Perhaps it is the elderberry?

No, for the elderberry is the most fussy of the fruits.

Perhaps it is the nectarine?

No, for the nectarine is the most sartorial of the fruits.

Is it the juniper berry?

No, for the juniper berry is the most cunning of the fruits.

Is it the watermelon?

No, for the watermelon is the most extrovert of the fruits.

Then is it the pomegranate?

No, for the pomegranate is the most macabre of the fruits.

Then is it the star fruit?

No, for the star fruit is the most wilful of the fruits.

Perhaps it is the date?

No, for the date is the most punctual of the fruits.

Perhaps it is the coconut?

No, for the coconut is the most lenient of the fruits.

Is it the lychee?

No, for the lychee is the most flirtatious of the fruits.

Is it the gooseberry?

No, for the gooseberry is the most intrusive of the fruits.

Then is it the mandarin?

No, for the mandarin is the most feudal of the fruits.

Then is it the kiwi fruit?

No, for the kiwi fruit is the most poetic of the fruits.

So it is the banana!

Yes! For the banana is the fruit in the bowl that smiles.

2   The Vegetables

Which is the most intelligent of the vegetables?

Is it asparagus?

No, for asparagus is the most aloof of the vegetables.

Is it green beans?

No, for green beans are the most parochial of the vegetables.

Then is it carrots?

No, for carrots are the most perceptive of the vegetables.

Then is it dill?

No, for dill is the most confused of the vegetables.

Perhaps it is kale?

No, for kale is the most derivative of the vegetables.

Perhaps it is lettuce?

No, for lettuce is the most sluggish of the vegetables.

Is it broccoli?

No, for broccoli is the most bored of the vegetables.

Is it haricot beans?

No, for haricot beans are the most pretentious of the vegetables.

Then is it iceberg lettuce?

No, for iceberg lettuce is the most trivial of the vegetables.

Then is it onions?

No, for onions are the most attention-seeking of the vegetables.

Perhaps it is spinach?

No, for spinach is the most relaxed of the vegetables.

Perhaps it is endive?

No, for endive is the most over-dressed of the vegetables.

Is it mangetout?

No, for mangetout is the most bossy of the vegetables.

Is it turnip?

No, for turnip is the most spooky of the vegetables.

Then is it Jerusalem artichokes?

No, for Jerusalem artichokes are the most stubborn of the vegetables.

Then is it peas?

No, for peas are the most polite of the vegetables.

Perhaps it is fennel?

No, for fennel is the most bohemian of the vegetables.

Perhaps it is rocket?

No, for rocket is the most effete of the vegetables.

Is it watercress?

No, for watercress is the most ornamental of the vegetables.

Is it new potatoes?

No, for new potatoes are the most childish of the vegetables.

Then is it zucchini?

No, for zucchini are the most bilingual of the vegetables.

Then is it yam?

No, for yam is the most calm of the vegetables.

So it is the cauliflower!

Yes! For the cauliflower is the vegetable in the rack with a brain.

3   The Flowers

Which is the most besotted of the flowers?

Is it the buttercup?

No, for the buttercup is the most nostalgic of the flowers.

Is it the daffodil?

No, for the daffodil is the most literary of the flowers.

Then is it the poppy?

No, for the poppy is the most bereaved of the flowers.

Then is it jasmine?

No, for jasmine is the most sophisticated of the flowers.

Perhaps it is the lily?

No, for the lily is the most ceremonial of the flowers.

Perhaps it is the fuchsia?

No, for the fuchsia is the most expectant of the flowers.

Is it the anemone?

No, for the anemone is the most paranoid of the flowers.

Is it the orchid?

No, for the orchid is the most heartbroken of the flowers.

Then is it the tulip?

No, for the tulip is the most artistic of the flowers.

Then is it the snapdragon?

No, for the snapdragon is the most hospitable of the flowers.

Perhaps it is the lupin?

No, for the lupin is the most vigilant of the flowers.

Perhaps it is the crocus?

No, for the crocus is the most reliable of the flowers.

Is it the thistle?

No, for the thistle is the most patriotic of the flowers.

Is it the hollyhock?

No, for the hollyhock is the most homesick of the flowers.

Then is it the chrysanthemum?

No, for the chrysanthemum is the most pompous of the flowers.

Then is it the violet?

No, for the violet is the most devoted of the flowers.

Perhaps it is gladioli?

No, for gladioli are the most pleased of the flowers.

Perhaps it is the foxglove?

No, for the foxglove is the most dexterous of the flowers.

Is it japonica?

No, for japonica is the most meditative of the flowers.

Is it the iris?

No, for the iris is the most watchful of the flowers.

Then is it the wallflower?

No, for the wallflower is the most hopeful of the flowers.

Then is it the snowdrop?

No, for the snowdrop is the most truthful of the flowers.

Perhaps it is the marigold?

No, for the marigold is the most confident of the flowers.

Perhaps it is the petunia?

No, for the petunia is the most timid of the flowers.

Is it the geranium?

No, for the geranium is the most predictable of the flowers.

Is it the daisy?

No, for the daisy is the most sociable of the flowers.

Then is it the sunflower?

No, for the sunflower is the most inspiring of the flowers.

So it is the rose!

Yes! For the rose is the flower in the garden of love.

4   The Trees

Which is the most hilarious of the trees?

Is it the oak?

No, for the oak is the most loyal of the trees.

Is it the weeping willow?

No, for the weeping willow is the most sensitive of the trees.

Then is it the poplar?

No, for the poplar is the most gossipy of the trees.

Then is it the silver birch?

No, for the silver birch is the most magical of the trees.

Perhaps it is the horse chestnut?

No, for the horse chestnut is the most playful of the trees.

Perhaps it is the ash?

No, for the ash is the most addictive of the trees.

Is it the elm?

No, for the elm is the most quizzical of the trees.

Is it the fir?

No, for the fir is the most jovial of the trees.

Then is it the yew?

No, for the yew is the most vocational of the trees.

Then is it the larch?

No, for the larch is the most kind of the trees.

Perhaps it is the Judas tree?

No, for the Judas tree is the most unreliable of the trees.

Perhaps it is the beech?

No, for the beech is the most zany of the trees.

Is it the palm tree?

No, for the palm tree is the most protective of the trees.

Is it the rowan?

No, for the rowan is the most querulous of the trees.

Then is it the ginkgo?

No, for the ginkgo is the most superior of the trees.

Perhaps it is the Douglas fir?

No, for the Douglas fir is the most clannish of the trees.

Perhaps it is the elder?

No, for the elder is the most experienced of the trees.

Is it the iroko?

No, for the iroko is the most fearless of the trees.

Is it the cedar?

No, for the cedar is the most grandiose of the trees.

Then is it the handkerchief tree?

No, for the handkerchief tree is the most solicitous of the trees.

Then is it the teak?

No, for the teak is the most yielding of the trees.

Perhaps it is the little nut tree?

No, for the little nut tree is the most fabulous of the trees.

Perhaps it is the alder?

No, for the alder is the most anecdotal of the trees.

So it is the monkey puzzle tree!

Yes! For the monkey puzzle tree is the funniest tree in the forest.

RAN OUT
OF SUGAR

Ran out of sugar – went next door,
asked the cat for a cup. Can't,
she purred, run out of cream.
Teamed up – went next door, asked
the dog for a jug. No way, he barked,
run out of tea. So we poor three
went next door, asked the cow
for a caddy. Can't, she mooed,
run out of toast. Four strong,
we went next door, asked the fox
for a loaf. Can't, he drawled, run out
of butter. Five now, went next door,

asked the sheep for a pat. Can't, she baaed,
run out of jam. Formed a gang and went next door,
asked the pig for a jar. Can't, he squealed,
run out of honey. Wasn't funny. Went next door,
asked the horse for a comb. Nay, he neighed,
run out of eggs. Thirty legs went next door,
asked the goat for a carton. Can't, he cursed,
run out of bacon. Nine now, went next door
and asked the rat for a rasher. Can't, he spat,
run out of sausage. Ten proud, went next door,
asked the hare for a link. Can't, he lisped,
run out of mustard. First XI went next door,
asked the hen for a scrape. Can't, she clucked,
run out of pepper. Dozen of us went next door,
asked the mouse for a mill. Can't, she squeaked,
run out of soup. Formed a line, went next door,
asked the mule for a bowl. Can't, he brayed,
run out of cake. Went next door, asked the bull
for a slice. Can't, he snorted, run out of ale.
Fifty-six legs trailed next door, asked the frog
for a pint. Can't, he croaked, run out of nuts.
Fifteen tuts. Went next door. We were back
at mine. Still no sugar. Ran out of wine.

MOON

Scotland's moon
came up like a warrior's bronze shield
over the giant concrete and glass
of the new high-rise.

One hand made a fist
where a hard round coin
sweated its copper
into my skin.

The other
held onto my father's mother's hand.
Armstrong took
his one small step for a man

250,000 miles
over our heads –
or in a Hollywood studio,
as Grandma scornfully said.

HAIKUS
FROM BASHO

1

In rainy weather
even the cheeky monkey
needs an umbrella.

2

From the ancient pond
with a spring and leap and splash
burps a new green frog.

3

When friends say goodbye
forever, it's like wild geese
erased by the clouds.

4

I gaze at the moon.
Without the gathering clouds
I would hurt my neck.

5

Tall summer grasses
stand at ease now in the fields
where the soldiers fell.

6

The pale butterfly
gently perfumes her frail wings
in an orchid bath.

7

This lonely poet
walks down a long empty road
into autumn dusk.

8

The morning after
the night before, the firefly
is only a bug.

THE RINGS

With this ring of lead
I me wed
to grey skies, rainfall, writing days.

With this wooden ring
I me wed
to forests, grim tales, ancient things.

With this ring of stone
I me wed
to mountains, echoes, vanishings.

With this silver ring
I me wed
to rivers, moonlight, midnight hours.

With this ring of gold
I me wed
to meadows, sunsets, wishing wells.

With this ruby ring
I me wed
to passion, poems, magic spells.

THE HAT

I was on Chaucer's head when he said He was a verray,
parfit gentil knyght, and tossed me into the air. I landed
on Thomas Wyatt's hair as he thought They fle from me
that sometyme did me seek, then left me behind in an Inn.
Sir Philip Sidney strolled in, picked me up, saying
My true love hath my hart and I have his, then hoopla'd me
straight onto William Shakespeare's head as he said
Tell me where is fancie bred, and passed me along
to John Donne, who was wearing me as he sang Go
and catch a falling star, but handed me on to one leaving
the bar, name of Herbert, George, who wore me up top
like a halo, murmured Love bade me welcome, yet my soul
drew back, then lay me dreamily down at the end of a pew
in a church. I was there for a while, dwelling on heaven
and hell, till Andrew Marvell arrived, said Had we
but World enough and Time, and filled me up to the brim

with blooms to give to a girl. She kept the flowers,
but handed me on to warm the crown of a balding chap,
named Milton, John, who sported me the day he happened
to say They also serve who only stand and wait,
then threw me over a gate. I fell in the path of Robert Herrick,
who scooped me up with a shout of Gather ye rosebuds
while ye may! and later gave me away to Dryden, John,
who tried me on for size, saying None but the brave
deserves the fair, then let me drop. I was soon picked up
by a bloke, Alexander Pope, who admitted the gen'ral rule
that every poet's a fool with cheerful grace, then tilted me
over the face of Christopher Smart, who loved his cat, said
For first he looks upon his forepaws to see if they
are clean, and let the kitty kip in myself, The Hat. I was saved
from that by William Blake, who liked the extra inch or two
I gave to his height as he bawled out Tyger, Tyger, burning
bright in the forests of the night, then bartered me
for the price of a mutton pie to Robbie Burns, who stared
in the mirror, grunted O, wad some Pow'r the giftie gie us
to see oursels as others see us! and threw me out
of the window. S. T. Coleridge passed, muttering Water,
water, everywhere, nor any drop to drink, and bore me
off to the Lakes to give as a gift to Wordsworth. Will

wore me to keep out the cold on a stroll when, all at once,
he said that he saw a crowd, a host of golden daffodils,
and lobbed me high with delight! It was late at night
when Byron came, mad, bad, bit of a lad, insisting So,
we'll go no more a roving, as he kicked me into a tree.
A breeze blew me gently down from my branch to flop
onto Shelley's head as he said O, Wind, if Winter comes,
can Spring be far behind? But Keats sneaked up,
snatched me away, wore me the night he claimed
I cannot see what flowers are at my feet, and left me
snagged on a bush in the gathering dark of a park.
John Clare came along, shouted I am, yet what I am
none cares or knows, and jammed me down
on his puzzled brow as he made for the open road.
Then Tennyson, Alfred, Lord, thundered past on a horse
and yanked me off, yelled Into the Valley of Death
rode the six hundred! I flew from his head as he galloped
away, and settled on Browning's crown as he said This
to you – my moon of poets, and got down on one knee
to present Little Me to Elizabeth Barrett. I liked it up there,
snug on her shiny hair, as she cooed How do I love thee,
let me count the ways, but she handed me down
for Emily Brontë to wear on the moors as she wailed
Fifteen wild Decembers from those brown hills have melted

into Spring, then a blast of wind blew me to the edge of the sea
where Matthew Arnold wore me to keep off the spray
when he said Listen! You hear the grating roar of pebbles
which the waves draw back, and lobbed me over the foam
like a boy with a stone. I bobbed away like a boat,
till fished from the drink on t'other side of the pond
by Whitman, Walt, who wrung me dry and flung me high
as he bawled Behold, I do not give lectures or a little
charity, when I give I give myself, and sent me on with a kiss
to Emily Dickinson. She popped me into a hat-box, along
with a note that read This is my letter to the world,
that never wrote to me, then posted me over land and sea
to Christina Rossetti, who used me to keep the blazing sun
from her face as she asked Does the road wind up-hill
all the way? The reply being yes, she considered it best
to hand me to Hopkins, Gerard Manley, whose head
I adorned as he warmly intoned Glory be to God
for dappled things, but I fell to the ground as he stared
at the sky. Thomas Hardy came sauntering by, spied me
and tried me, said I am the family face; flesh perishes,
I live on, and tossed me to one who stood on his own
by a tree – Housman, A. E. He sported me, saying Lads
in their hundreds to Ludlow come in for the fair, but lost me,
while arm-wrestling there in a bar, to Kipling, Rudyard,

who fiddled with me the day he pronounced If you can meet
with triumph and disaster and treat those two impostors
just the same, then carelessly left me behind in the back
of a cab. Next in was an Irish chap, W. B. Yeats, who gave
the driver a tip, carried me off to wear at a tilt on his head
as he said Tread softly because you tread on my dreams,
so Charlotte Mew bore me away, murmured no year
has been like this that has just gone by, and started to cry.
A train sighed by. Edward Thomas leaned out, said
Yes, I remember Adlestrop, and lifted me up, but a cold wind
blew me Wilfred Owen's way; he turned me sadly round
and around in his hands and asked What passing-bells
for these who die as cattle? then hurled me back
at the wind. I was seized as I flew by Ezra Pound,
who wore me out and about, saying Winter is
icummen in, Lhude sing Goddamn! then posted me
into the safety deposit box of the bank where T. S. Eliot
worked. April, he said, is the cruellest month, and used me
to keep off the rain, leaving me lying behind on a bench
when the sun came out. I was found by MacDiarmid, Hugh,
and was warming the egg of his head when he said I'll ha'e
nae hauf-way hoose, but aye be whaur extremes meet –
then dropped me down at the feet of Lawrence, D. H.,
who picked me up and was modelling me as he mused

I never saw a wild thing sorry for itself, then chucked me over
to Robert Graves. He pulled me low on his head and said
There's a cool web of language winds us in, then began
to nod off. I was pinched from his brow by Riding, Laura,
who was trying me on as she thought The wind suffers
of blowing, the sea suffers of water, then squashed me
down onto Dylan Thomas's curls. Do not, he said.
go gentle into that good night, then sold me on
for the price of a pint to Louis MacNeice. He wore
when he said World is crazier and more of it
than we think, then decided to give me to Auden, W. H.
He was delighted, wore me all night, said the desires
of the heart are as crooked as corkscrews, but left me
behind the next day in the loo. John Betjeman found me,
smoothed, dusted-down me, and popped me on
as he trilled Come, friendly bombs, then flopped me on
to the head of Philip Larkin, who cycled past, saying
Man hands on misery to man, then stopped at a church
and handed me on by the graves to Stevie Smith,
who wore me on holiday with her aunt, where she said
I was much further out than you thought, and not waving
but drowning. I was all at sea, till Elizabeth Bishop deftly
hooked me, said I caught a tremendous fish, and held him
beside the boat, then left me behind on an airport seat

for Robert Lowell to find and put on for the flight over
to England. He arrived and declared Everywhere,
giant finned cars nose forward like fish, and gave me
to Sylvia Plath. Dying, she said, is an art like everything else,
and left me to Hughes, Ted, man in black, who growled
with a sudden sharp hot stink of fox it enters the dark hole
of the head . . . but whose head, whose head, whose head,
whose head, whose head, whose will I settle on next?

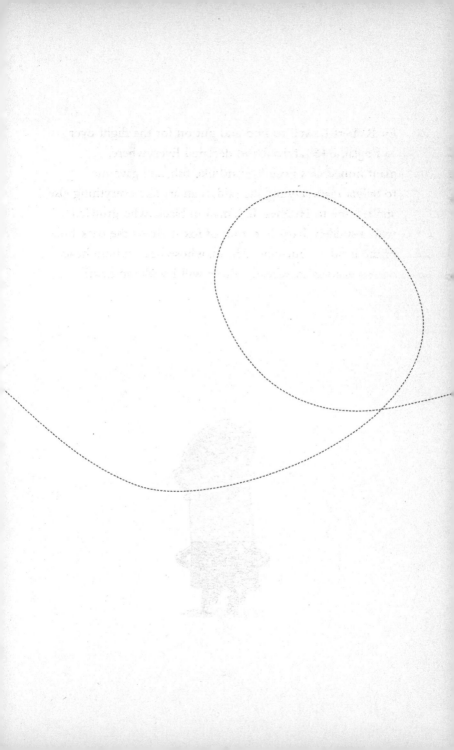